The Bin Bears

Scoular Anderson

CORGI PUPS

To Francesca

Series reading consultant: Prue Goodwin,
Reading and Language Information Centre,
University of Reading

THE BIN BEARS
A CORGI PUPS BOOK

First publication in Great Britain

PRINTING HISTORY
Corgi Pups edition published 2001

ISBN 0 552 54946 0

Set in 18/25 pt Bembo MT Schoolbook

Corgi Pups Books are published by Transworld Publishers,
61–63 Uxbridge Road, Ealing, London W5 5SA,
a division of the Random House Group Ltd,
in Australia by Random House Australia (Pty) Ltd,
20 Alfred Street, Milsons Point, Sydney, NSW 2061, Australia
in New Zealand by Random House New Zealand Ltd,
18 Poland Road, Glenfield, Auckland 10, New Zealand
and in South Africa by Random House (Pty) Ltd,
Endulini, 5a Jubilee Road, Parktown 2193, South Africa

Printed and bound in Denmark by
Nørhaven Paperback, Viborg

Contents

Chapter 1

The bin truck went down the road.

Clank, clatter, thump, roar!

The bin men
picked up bags.

They lifted bins.

They pushed wheelie bins.

One of the bin men saw
something lying on the ground.
It was a toy dinosaur and it had
fallen out of a bin. The bin man
picked it up and gave it a clean
on his overalls. "Funny-looking
thing!" he said.

The bin man took the dinosaur round to the front of the truck. He stuck the dinosaur on the radiator. "There!" he said. "You can be our new mascot!"

Three pairs of eyes turned
and looked at the dinosaur.

The three pairs of eyes belonged
to three bears.

"I thought *we* were the bin
truck mascots," said Dusty Bear.

"It's got no ears or fur!" said
Threadbare Bear.

"You're a funny-looking
bear!" said Posh Bear.

"I'm not a bear, I'm a dinosaur. I'm Dotty the Dinosaur," said the dinosaur.

"Well, we're the Bin Bears," said Posh Bear, "so you must be a *Bino*-saur!"

And the Bin Bears laughed at this joke so much that they almost fell off the truck.

Dotty looked annoyed but inside, she had a laugh trying to get out.

She couldn't hold it in any
longer and laughed along with
the Bin Bears.

The four mascots were still
laughing when the bin truck got
back to the depot.

The driver backed the bin truck into the shed. The gates were closed and the bin men went home.

"'Night!" said Fred.

"See you!" said Jim.

"Cheers!" said Leo.

"Bye!" said Mick.

The sun began to set. "It will soon be dark and we can go out and have some fun," said Posh Bear.

"I don't feel like fun," said Dotty. "My people have just thrown me out!"

"That's the trouble with people," said Posh Bear. "They grow bigger, then they forget about you. I was left to sit on a window-sill for three years. It was so boring."

"My people gave me to the dog to play with," said Threadbare Bear.

"My people shut me up in the loft for years," said Dusty Bear. He gave himself a shake and the dust flew out in clouds.

"*I* had to hold up a pile of books," said Dotty.

"People think you should just sit there for ever," said Posh Bear. "But now we're retired we have lots of FUN!"

"Like what?" asked Dotty.

"We run around," said Dusty Bear.

"We find things for our collection," said Threadbare Bear.

"We might find a coin or a
glove or a football," said Posh
Bear.

The Bears jumped down from
the truck.

"Come on, Dotty, jump!" said
Posh Bear.

Dotty jumped.

Then the Bin Bears ran towards
a hole in the gate. They jumped
through and danced off down
the road. By the time Dotty
caught up with the Bears
they were already having fun
jumping in puddles.

However, the Bears didn't know that their greatest enemy was nearby. Old Fleakeeper the cat was hiding between two cars.

"Now I'll get these silly bears!" he said to himself, as he got ready to pounce.

Just as Fleakeeper jumped, the
Bears jumped, too . . .

. . . and Fleakeeper got a good
soaking.

SPLOSH!

The Bears ran for it and
Dotty found herself alone. She
wasn't quite alone, though, as a
dark shadow fell across the
place where she was standing.

But just as Fleakeeper was
about to pounce there was a
loud noise. "Woof woof woof!"

Fleakeeper turned and ran but there was no pack of dogs around, only the Bears making barking noises.

After that scare the Bears rushed Dotty back to the depot. "If this is your idea of fun," she said, "I'd rather be at the bottom of a bin!"

Chapter 3

In the morning the depot gates were opened and the bin truck drove down Clover Road to start another day's work.

The Bin Bears watched from the front of their truck. They knew everything that went on in the town.

"The people at number 37 have a new car," said Threadbare Bear.

"The woman at 43 is late for work. She should be at the bus stop by now," said Posh Bear.

"Oh, look!" said Posh Bear. "The curtains are still closed in the room above the door of number 60."

"The little girl in there always waves to us," said Dusty.

"And it's her birthday soon," said Threadbare.

"How do you know that?" asked Dotty.

"We saw her dad hiding a new bike in the garage," said Posh Bear.

"And we saw a large cake being delivered," said Dusty.

"I bet we see the postman
deliver lots of cards soon," said
Posh Bear. "And look! There's
the doctor coming out of the
house now."

"The little girl must be ill!"
said Dusty. "Just before her
birthday, too!"

As the bin truck drew level
with number 60 Clover Road,
a pale face peered round the
curtains. The little girl gave a
wave and the Bears gave an
extra big wave back.

That night, when the bin truck was back in the depot, Dusty Bear said, "I wish we had a present for the little girl."

Then Posh Bear had an idea.

"Listen, Dotty, I think we should get you into number 60. You would make a lovely present for the little girl."

"Yes!" said Threadbare Bear.

"Brilliant!" said Dusty Bear.

Dotty looked pleased.

"Let's get going, then!" said Posh Bear.

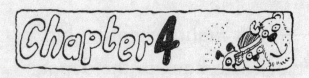

Chapter 4

"The first thing we have to do is clean you up a bit," said Posh Bear. "So follow me!"

The Bears ran to the bottom of the street and stopped outside a launderette. Threadbare Bear pushed aside a bit of wood and they crawled in.

Once they were in the launderette
they waited in a dark corner.

"What's going to happen?"
asked Dotty.

"Aha!" said the Bears. "Wait
and see!" Just then, the door of
the launderette opened.

Someone came in with a bag of washing.

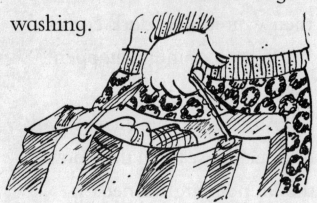

The Bears grabbed Dotty and threw her into the washing bag.

Then they sat and waited while
the washing was put into the
machine . . .

. . . and Dotty was washed . . .

. . . and rinsed . . .

. . . and spun.

Dotty knew she had to escape
as soon as the wash was over
but she was so dizzy when she
was lifted out of the machine
she couldn't do anything.

She was spotted. "What's this,
then?" said the owner of the
washing.

"You're a funny-looking
little thing! I reckon
you've fallen out of
someone else's
pocket in the
wash! I'll
leave you
here in case someone comes
back to look for you."

She put Dotty on a high ledge
above the washing machines.

Chapter 5

The Bears woke up when they heard the door of the launderette closing. They ran out of their hiding place, but couldn't see Dotty anywhere.

Then they heard a little voice
calling high above their heads.

"Don't worry, Dotty!" said
Posh Bear. "We'll get you down
somehow!"

"I see just the thing!" said
Posh Bear and he began to pull
a plastic bag out of a corner. "If
we hold this out, Dotty can
jump onto it," he said.

The Bears stretched the bag
out and held it tight.

"Jump, Dotty!" shouted Posh
Bear.

It did seem a long way down but Dotty closed her eyes and jumped.

Down she flew . . .

. . . onto the bag . . .

. . . then up again.

When Dotty stopped
bouncing the Bears carried her
out of the launderette.

Once they were safely back
in the depot, the Bears could
admire the beautifully clean
Dotty.

"The only thing is," said Dotty sadly, "if I'm going to be a birthday present I ought to be wrapped in paper and tied with ribbon."

"Oh, we've plenty of that sort of thing," said Posh Bear. "Follow me!"

The Bears ran to the back of
the shed and squeezed through a
hole in the floor.

By the light of a street lamp,
Dotty saw a huge pile of things
hidden under the floor of the
shed.

"What's all this?" she asked.

"It's our collection," said Posh Bear. "It's amazing what people drop!" said Dusty Bear.

"It's amazing what people lose," said Threadbare Bear.

"It's amazing what people throw away, and all as good as new," said Posh Bear. "And we find it!"

There were shoes and gloves
and pens and toy cars. There
were packets of sweets and tea-
bags and earrings. There were
balloons and streamers and bits
of tinsel.

"This is just what we need!"
said Dotty.

The Bears ran around collecting things. Dusty Bear wrapped Dotty up in coloured paper.

Threadbare Bear
tied some ribbon
round her.

Posh Bear placed a crown of
tinsel on her head. Dotty was
ready to go.

"We'll have to hurry," said
Dusty Bear. "It'll be daylight
soon."

"We'll use the trolley," said Posh Bear. "We'll get there quicker."

Dusty Bear and Threadbare Bear ran to a corner of the yard and came back with a supermarket trolley. They loaded up the trolley with boxes and helped Dotty up on top.

"What are the boxes for?" she
asked.

"Aha!" said the Bears. "Wait
and see!"

They gave the trolley a little
push, then jumped on. They
were on their way. Down the
hill they sped. The Bears yelled
with delight.

At the bottom of the hill,
Fleakeeper heard them coming.
"This time, I'll get them," he
said to himself. Fleakeeper leapt
out from his hiding place . . .

. . . but ended up getting soaked
again.

Chapter 6

The Bears stopped the trolley
outside Number 60 Clover
Road.

"How am I to get inside?"
Dotty asked.

"Don't worry, we've thought
of that," said Posh Bear.

Threadbare Bear lifted a plank
of wood from the trolley.

Dusty Bear brought an empty
paint can.

"I hope you don't
mind flying,
Dotty," said
Posh Bear.

The Bears used the plank and
can to make a seesaw.

"You're going to stand on one
end," said Posh Bear. "We're
going to jump onto the other
end and up you will go onto
that window ledge."

Dotty wasn't very keen on this idea. "Wouldn't you like to come with me?" she asked.

"We're a bit scruffy," said Threadbare Bear.

"We're a bit wild," said Dusty Bear.

"Thanks, but we like it where we are," said Posh Bear.

So Dotty climbed onto the plank and the Bears climbed onto a ledge.

"It's goodbye for now, Dotty," said Posh Bear.

"Good luck!" said Threadbare Bear.

"See you around!" said Dusty Bear.

Dotty closed her eyes and waited. The three bears jumped. Dotty flew upwards like a rocket.

The world seemed to turn
upside down.

She landed safely on the window
-sill. The window was open so
she crept into her new home.

The Bears went back into the street and lifted the boxes from the trolley. They carried them back into the garden of number 60 and climbed into a tree.

They had just one more thing to do before going home.

The next day, inside number 60, the little girl began to open her presents – a beautiful bike, clothes, books, sweets.

Dotty could hardly wait for her own wrapping paper to be taken off.

When the little girl saw the dinosaur, she gave a big smile and kissed Dotty.

Just then, there was a
rumbling noise outside. The bin
truck was coming down Clover
Road.

"Let's go and wave to the
Bears!" said the little girl and
she ran to the window with
Dotty . . . and outside there was
yet another surprise . . .

. . . and everyone in the street
was admiring it.

Dotty was very happy in her new home. At night, when she heard a can rattling in the street or a cat screeching, she thought of the Bin Bears having their fun . . .

. . . and every morning, as the bin truck went down Clover Road on the way to work, the Bears gave Dotty a big wave.

THE END